And Sometimes Y

Written by Jason Elias

Illustrated by Kevin Scott Collier

Publishers Cataloging-in-Publication Data

Elias, Jason.
    And sometimes Y / written by Jason Elias ; illustrated by Kevin
Scott Collier.
      p. cm.
    Summary: All the letters in Alphabet Village live peacefully together,
until Y is forced to choose between being a consonant or a vowel.
    ISBN-13: 978-1-60131-066-8
    [1. Alphabet. 2. Alphabet—Juvenile fiction. 3. Consonants.
4. Vowels.] I. Collier, Kevin Scott, ill. II. Title.

                              2009940331

115 Bluebill Drive
Savannah, GA 31419
United States
(888) 300-1961

This book was published with the assistance of the helpful folks at DragonPencil.com

To Colin and Aidan:

You raise me up.

After 98 years, nothing had changed in Alphabet Village.
As was the tradition on the eve of every new year,
the residents of the village gathered by the great clock
next to the Bridge of Friendship.

The capital letters
brought their baby
lowercase letters to
the bridge. The capitals
looked upon their babies
as any proud parent would
look upon a young letter.

Vowels from the West and consonants from the East walked, skipped, and ran toward the festive gathering to sing the Alphabet Song together. The sweet harmony could be heard for miles, just as it had been for almost a century.

All the letters rejoiced and sang: "A and B,
Or X, Y, Z—
They are all the same
To you and me.

Consonants and Vowels,
Upper- or Lowercase–
We all make up
The great Alphabet Race."

Roman Numeral I, the mayor of the neighboring village, Number Town, stepped forward to speak as an honorary guest after the singing stopped. He spoke loudly, "Thank you for inviting me to the 99th Anniversary of Alphabet Village. Your peaceful, happy village

is everything that we, in Number Town, wish to be. I want to wish you a Happy New Year and a wonderful year to come."

Fireworks exploded in the air, and beautiful colors filled the sky. Everyone was happy, and they ended the festivities by singing the Alphabet Song:

"A and B,
Or X, Y, Z–
They are all the same
To you and me.

Consonants and Vowels,
Upper- or Lowercase–
We all make up
The great Alphabet Race."

As the town's letters went toward their homes, something strange happened. A stray question mark approached the Y family and asked, "Are you vowels or consonants?"

Every letter stopped. No one knew the answer. The Ys lived on the border of the vowel area of the West and the consonant area of the East. It never mattered to which group they belonged; letters were letters.

The eldest Y shouted, "Who cares?" and went home with the entire family of Y. This was the first bit of anger that Alphabet Village had ever seen.

The next day, the town was buzzing with the same question: "Are Ys consonants or vowels?" It began as a harmless question, but by the end of the week battle lines had been drawn. This once peaceful village had lost its love and happiness.

Mr. and Mrs. A called a gathering of all the vowels. They discussed how to win over the Y family to their side.

Mr. and Mrs. Z held a meeting of all consonants. They set up a campaign to make the Y family believe that they should be consonants.

Neither group of letters was permitted to speak to the other side. Love was quickly replaced by anger.

The two groups waited for an announcement from the
Y family. Would they be consonants or vowels?

Finally, the eldest Y spoke: "On New Year's Eve, the night that celebrates the end of the first century of our village, we will announce our decision. Until then, please leave us alone!"

The day finally arrived—the New Year's Eve of the 99th year. The traditional harmony of the previous 98 was gone, replaced with signs and chants supporting the two sides.

Roman Numeral I, the mayor of Number Town, walked to the podium just as he had the year before. This year, however, the mood of the crowd was noticeably different. He began, "What has happened to the peaceful, happy, loving village to which I spoke last year?"

The eldest Y explained, "They are making us choose whether we want to be vowels or consonants. Tonight is the night we must announce our decision."

Roman Numeral I asked sadly, "Why must you choose?
Don't you remember your song?"

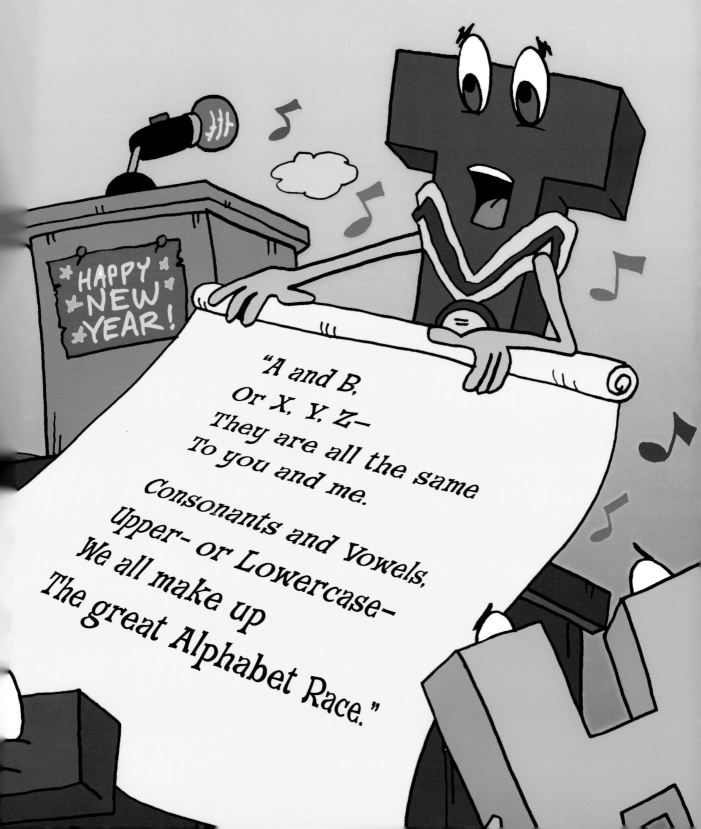

At that moment, the chants of vowels and consonants ceased. Mr. and Mrs. A and Mr. and Mrs. Z looked across the Friendship Bridge, which now stood between them. They began to sing the song they sang for the previous 98 New Year's Eves, and the whole town joined them:

"A and B,   Consonants and Vowels,
Or X, Y, Z–   Upper- or Lowercase–
They are all the same   We all make up
To you and me.   The great Alphabet Race."

The Y family thanked Roman Numeral I for solving the problem. Eldest Y proclaimed, "Every Y has two paths. We can always be a consonant, but when vowels need us, the rule can be 'A, E, I, O, U, AND SOMETIMES Y!!!'"

Alphabet Village rejoiced and returned to its peaceful, happy, and loving ways.

Words with Y

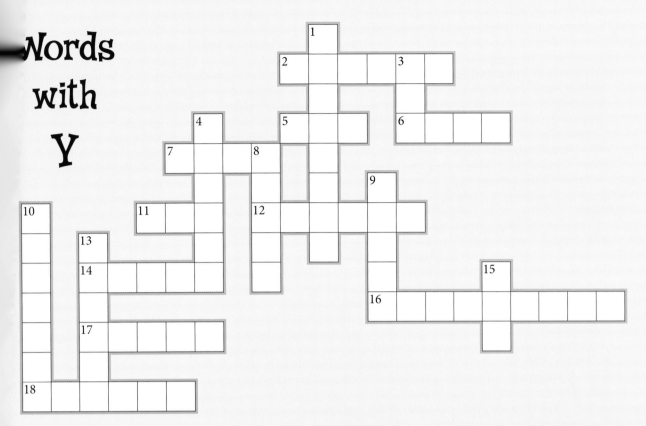

Across

2. not ugly
5. opposite of no
6. when tired you _____
7. 365 days
11. the organ that helps you see
12. a cowardly color
14. not sad
16. a large room for athletic activity
17. a leafy spice
18. something representing something else

Down

1. to be nice to another person
3. to make an effort
4. Many soups includes carrots and _____.
8. king and queen, the _____ family
9. not old
10. instrument that produces a sharp, ringing sound when struck
13. patterned recurrence of a beat
15. a large, stocky, shaggy-haired wild ox

JASON ELIAS is an English teacher by trade. *And Sometimes Y* is his first children's book. He loves teaching and coaching, but most of all he loves spending time with his family: his sons Colin and Aidan, and his wife Danielle. Jason graduated from Binghamton University '91, and received graduate degrees from Hofstra University and Queens College.

KEVIN SCOTT COLLIER is a published children's book author and illustrator with over 100 titles to his credit. His illustrated books have won contests and praise from New York Book Festival, The New York Times, The Hollywood Book Festival and World Magazine. Collier also appears weekly as an illustrator/instructor on the KICKS Club television show, which broadcasts around the world on several Christian Television networks. He lives with his wife and son in Grand Haven, Michigan.